I0727036

*For Bea, Nancy and Theo
in their Poetry Room*

www.1889books

ISBN:978-1-915045-20-1

The Skittery Zipper

and other poems for children of all ages

Michael Glover & Ruth Dupré

The Skittery Zipper

That blue dog's ghost on the horizon line —
Did it notice the signal? Did it shine in its eyes?

Some dust fell into the blue dog's eyes.
It made him blind, oh, it made him blind.

When I first saw his ghost on the horizon line,
I whistled and called. I whistled and cried:

Blue dog, bulky boy, skittery zipper,
Look into my eyes, let's live forever...

Now nothing shines in the blue dog's eyes.
A cloud of dust has made him blind.

The blue dog jumps, and the blue dog falls.
It's all I remember. The rest is this wall,

Where I lean and imagine his bulk and his size —
No bigger than a tin can stoked with fire.

Now the blue dog's gone from the horizon line.
A truck hauled him off to the other side.

Give me that body, mr trucker man,
Let that body rest easy in these ghostly hands...

Blue dog, bulky boy, skittery zipper,
Stare into my eyes, let's live forever.

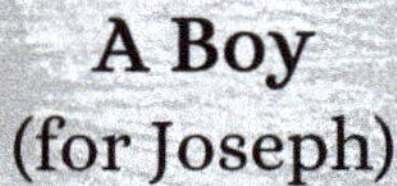

A Boy
(for Joseph)

Something has come at last of what we made.
This handsome, sturdy boy is craning round,
Taking the world in through his keen, small eyes.
His hands are grasping upwards, at some cloud.

I push him, with due patience, through the streets.
He tries to tell me what he feels. I nod.
He thanks me with a smile. I give it back.
The pushchair's lurching now: *a dog, a dog*!

I raise him up. He's blocking out the sun.
He squirms against my shoulder – o giant slug,
Don't disappear just yet into the grass.
Pulse with your vital life upon this rug.

A Boy
(for Joseph)

Something has come at last of what we made.
This handsome, sturdy boy is craning round,
Taking the world in through his keen, small eyes.
His hands are grasping upwards, at some cloud.

I push him, with due patience, through the streets.
He tries to tell me what he feels. I nod.
He thanks me with a smile. I give it back.
The pushchair's lurching now: *a dog, a dog*!

I raise him up. He's blocking out the sun.
He squirms against my shoulder – o giant slug,
Don't disappear just yet into the grass.
Pulse with your vital life upon this rug.

The Problem Child

I live alone with a problem child.
The problem child is not my child.
We share one bed, one bath, one book.
The child shares nothing. He is wild.

I found the child on a winter's day.
The street was newly dressed with snow.
The child stood with his back to me,
An orange circle by his toe.

The problem child stared at the ground.
I took his arm. He flung it off.
I tried such talk as I could find.
It wasn't much. My mouth was locked.

O problem child, what is your name?
I have no name. I am myself.
O problem child, where are you from?
From Nowhere Town, by way of Stealth.

I live alone with a problem child.
The day is grey, taut as this string.
I pace the room. I clatter pans.
Sometimes he cries. Sometimes we sing.

A Sunken World

I am the smallest of the lost continents.
I sank beneath the sea the day your back was turned.
Now, when you look out upon that great expanse of waters,
It is just as if I have never been —
Seagulls float and skim so easily above the place where I sank;
The winds comb the waters as if they have nothing to hide
    and nothing to reveal...

I have no idea what I shall do down here
During the aeons of time which lie ahead of me.
Plants will grow upon me at their whim,
Upon which tiny suckerfish will doubtless feed.

Every decade or so a boat will settle down here to join me.
There will be no conversation between us.
No distant lost cries will reach me.
Frankly, there will be nothing to be said.

A Man called No One

A man called No One knocks at the door.
It is February time, a sharp snap of cold in every crevice.
Breath hangs in the air like old, thin curtains.
I am at a loose end, whether to stay or to go. Which.

It is then that No One calls, and I let him in
    with a modicum of ceremony.
I plump up the cushion and he settles, glad to be somewhere.
It is so easy for No One to be Nowhere.
He spends his lifetime in such parts, he tells me.
Until today, he mentions, when such a blessing
    fell from the air.

To be welcomed into the house of a stranger!
That the door should be unlatched,
    and the man turn as he enters!
Usually, he tells me, it is a matter of the blank-faced stare
And maybe a slight, uneasy shuffling of feet,
    which says just the one thing:
Something may be afoot here, but darned if I can say what it is.

I tell him then. I tell him straight.
I knew nothing of his coming.
The door was unlatched through a roaring fit of forgetfulness.
I have welcomed him into my house for want of anything better,
    that is the sad truth of it, I tell him.
We both sit opposite each other, heads hung, keening,
    like limp black tulips in a fluted vase.

The Song of the Three Fish

I saw three fish descend the stairs,
Arm in arm and devil-may-care,
Singing some old-time fish's song
Of cruel men with hooks and prongs

Who pitched and tossed on the bucking waves
In boats as tough as those men were brave,
And stabbed at long dead, helpless friends,
Hauling them forth on the prongs' sharp ends —

Such lean and comely fishermen,
All bronzed by toiling in the sun,
With fingers strong as an iron vise,
And eyes that flashed, and tongues of ice...

They sang and sang as down they came,
All wet from the sea and wildly gay.

Cold Street

I live on a street called Gladness.
There's always some hand reaching out.
My work takes me downhill, to Cold Street.
They're muffled down there. They don't talk.

It is hard for me to travel.
I live two quite separate lives.
The smiles that I use in the evening
The daylight people spit out.

I shall move one day to Cold Street.
For me, there is no other way.
It is where I must surely settle.
I have seen it every day.

I have seen them drift, as if dreaming,
Carrying all that they have —
A bundle of clothes and two blankets,
Looking so wretchedly sad.

From Gladness to sadness, they whisper.
Down Cold Street, they chant, every day:
This is where you must one day settle.
Come, child, there is no other way.

Big Sister Sue

My sister Sue lives in this room.
She sits and sits all day,
Just staring into empty space
And muttering away.

Mum feeds her with a spoon at meals.
The drool runs down her chin.
She's like a baby, but grown up.
Once she were small and thin.

I love her really, yes I do.
I've told me mum I do.
Mum says: *you give her all your love.*
She needs it all, poor little Sue...

And then mum cries, but I don't cry.
I kiss her on the arm.
I don't like mum to cry like that.
But dad says: do no harm...

Sometimes I get to push Sue's chair.
It's faster than you'd think.
It's really good down Bury Hill.
My sister Sue goes pink!

I love her, yes I really do.
I've told me mum I do.
But mum just says: *it's love she needs,*

You give it to our little Sue...

Anemone

She was called, I think, Anemone.
I wouldn't say I knew her well —
Scarcely at all.
She spoke, always, in an undertone.
She had grown very young again,
In a matter of months it seemed,
And very stooped and small.
She came to this door regularly.
She just stood there and waited —
For nothing at all.
I too waited, on my side, the inside,
For the fistfalls.
When they came, they were hard and brutal,
Three rough, rapid falls,
And then they stopped.
But if I didn't go
And talk to her,
Immediately open up my door,
She would wait out there for hours on end,
Not doing a thing, just breathing,
For a while, and then pretending to
Be something else — a dog or cat or something,
Anything with a small, insinuating call.
Anemone, I would say, speaking from the inside,
Please go away.
I need to do some work,
I cannot concentrate on anything at all
If you just stand out there and bawl.
I'm not bawling, she would say,
In a normalish sort of voice,
I'm not talking even.
I'm just sitting on this floor, out here,
Trying to be something sleek and thin
And even faintly beautiful.

The Dictator

A thousand thousand people know my name.
Ten thousand thousand use it every day.
A million children sing it in the streets.
A hundred widows weep my life away.

The banker's moistened thumbs caress my face.
The clouds arrange themselves into my shape.
The rivers babble of my deeds and dreams.
The monkey chatters of me in his cage.

The locomotives sigh for my lost loves.
God says: beside *this* man, I am mere stone and wood.
All arrows aim to pierce my heart's desire.
My armies march in flames. I am their fire.

The Mouse in the Statue

Where the god once lived,
There sleeps a mouse
Secure inside a tiny house
Of sawdust, sand and beetle dung...
His life there just goes on and on,
Serene and safe
From cats and snakes,
While priests patrol
The temple gates.

When the people come
They worship still,
Not knowing that
Their god is ill...
A mouse, eating its heart away,
Will bring it down to earth one day
And, once laid low,
It will not know
To resurrect itself
And go...

On a Mantelpiece, 1873

The cranky, red-faced baritone
Challenged the roof to rise a bit.
An old, old woman, hobbled, rude,
Addressed the fire with her spit.
The quiet one said: *I'm a fair maid
Of Staffordshire, whose father died...*
The young beau, her companion piece,
Suggested it was otherwise.
A farmer, whiskery and rouged,
Laughed suddenly – a thunderclap
That caused the mantelpiece to jolt
And all the figures to collapse
In bits upon the maple floor...

And that's the scene that met my eye
When I crept down the stairs at dawn
With spills, to jolly up the fire,
And set the breakfast things, through yawns.

My Girl Rwanda

My girl Rwanda,
Squatted by the fire,
Tossing in the little logs,
Make the flames go higher.

Where has mummy gone today?
Where has daddy been?
Why's he sitting in the dark,
Hand propping his chin?

Soon it will be night again.
Soon the goat man come
With a tinkle of his bell.
Then the children run.

But we don't run out today.
Daddy say: stay in!
Be no goatman hereabout.
Storm is rolling in.

But there is no black up there.
Neither sound of rain.
Blueness, blueness all the day,
Sunlight, plain as plain.

Still he say: don't you go out!
You just build the fire.
So I squat me here and watch
Flames go jumping higher.

Now the water steaming hard,
Water in the tub
Squatting on the flaming fire.
Soon I run and rub.

Daddy, bring the kangas here.
Toss them in the tub.
Rwanda wash the stains away.
See me rub and scrub.

An Invitation

Do come and see my special sea.
I've coloured it all grey.
There is no other colour now.
The others wore away.

There was a boat that sailed on it.
I pulled the plug. It drowned
With two red, waving men on board
Who loved to sing and lounge.

No, they weren't sailors, those two men.
They didn't mean to go.
It wasn't their boat that they sailed.
It came up from below.

They saw it on the beach today,
Just drifting with the tide.
They loved the gorgeous look of it,
That yellow hull, so smooth and wide...

Running to Heaven

Life runs away,
Going faster and faster.
You'd best get off
Or you'll never ever catch her!

Life runs away
In a blur of speed.
Screw your legs back on!
What else do you need?

Life runs away.
You've got to keep up!
You know you can do it.
It's yours, that Gold Cup.

The Broken Box

Somewhere there is a broken box
Inside that box there lives a man
A broken man in a broken box
Inside that man is a broken heart

Somewhere there is a broken world
Inside that world there is a land
A broken land in a broken world
Inside that land is a broken town

Somewhere there is a broken town
Inside that town there is a street
A broken street in a broken town
Along that street is a broken box.

I know that world with the broken land
I know that land with the broken town
I know that town with the broken street
I know that street with the broken box

I know that box with the broken man
I know that man with the broken heart
Inside my heart is that broken world
And all the rest is inside that

Bits and Pieces of a Morning

Bits and pieces on the table
Tea pot, plum tart, boggle-eyed beetle
Blue, grey, red in a plastic palette
And a thin violin new painted yellow

Bits and pieces on the table
All you need for a fresh day's journey
Pick up the pot and pour it out
Warming tea, straight from the spout!

A slice of tart to get you going
Crunchy at the outer edges
Just enough, but not too much…
Where's your coat? It's on its peg!

Paint the scene as quick as maybe
Play a tune – school morning's hurrying!
That beetle's ready for the journey –
Scratchy legs, twin headlamps blazing –

Hop on board and off you
scurry

The Kneeling King

The king goes up. The king goes down.
The king goes round and round and round.
His crown's too heavy for his head.
Let's make it out of paper then!

The king said: let's all kneel today,
And find a bird that's fast as light.
He chose a red one, yellow stripes,
And clutched it very, very tight…

You wait your hurry, were his words.
No bird flies off until I say.
The moment when the wind blows up,
That's when I'll let you fly away.

The king jumps up. The king kneels down.
The king goes round and round and round.
His crown's too heavy for his head.
Let's makes him out of paper then!

Just Sleeping

I slept the whole of yesterday.
And then I slept again today.
It's just so easy being asleep,
Watching a slide show of strange dreams.

That day you flew off from the roof
Or when I crossed the Irish Sea
On foot, with helicopters looking down
Or when mum made that sandwich big enough
To feed the poorest bit of town.

It's just so easy being asleep,
The way you drift and roam around,
Peering deep into people's lives
And seeing things you scarce believe –

That old man with the giant weights
Flinging a boulder at the moon…
Wasn't he that chap we used to know
Who lives in the Care Home down Blyde Road?

The Chocolate House

I said: I want to build a house
Of chocolate and marzipan
With a door of pink icing at the front.
I won't stop till I've made the roof.

You wait your hurry, little man!
You grow up first! You wait and see!
There's lots of learning to be done
From the likes of Dave and me.

I ate up all the chocolate books,
Six, seven, eight, nine, till I knew it all.
Marzipan came in leaflets, small,
That slid, so neat, between baby teeth.

One day when they were down the pub,
I found a little patch of ground
That no one had thought to build on yet,
A narrow plot, between tall trees.

It took about an hour, I'd say –
Sticky slabs make for an easy fit.
You should have seen their faces when
They rolled back, all those hissy fits!

See what he's done, the little scamp!
It's not for you, I said, it's mine.
I snapped the door knob off and licked.
The best bit was the chimney pot.

The Secret Reader

One day just slips into the next –
It's dark, it's light, it's in-between.
I never want to go to sleep.
It's just too interesting, what you see.

One night the mice played out for hours,
Dealing with food we'd left on plates,
Seven in a row, all going so fast.
The plates were clean by half past three.

But best is snooping on a dog
That always sleeps when you're awake.
Why does it jump when the lights go out,
And grab big books between its teeth?

The Stopped Clock

I'm waiting to begin again.
It won't be long. They promised me.
They stopped the clock at half past ten
When I was half way through a tease…

About this girl who wouldn't tell,
No matter what you bribed her with –
Chocolates, clothes, a wishing well.
She just stared at you, hard, and grinned.

I wanted to finish it all off,
And they were waiting, gritted teeth.
There was an answer to it all.
Then someone came, and the clock just stopped.

Not So Far

Not so far
So far to go
Said the dog in the tree
To the mole underground

Carrying only so much
As we're able
The dog with his basket
The mole with his whistle

Not so far
So far to go
Said the bird in the bush
To the tramp in the stable

Carrying only as much
As we're able
The bird with his ring
The tramp with his bundle

Not so far
So far to go
Said the legs to the feet
And the tired to the hungry

Carrying only as much
As we're able
A basket of hope
And a tumble of wishes

Wednesdays

Wednesdays always happen on a Wednesday,
Every week without stopping.
Sometimes I paint the sky a thin grey,
At other times a thick, smeary yellow.

Wednesday is always half way between,
Far enough from horrible Monday
When it's only ever lessons,
But close enough to brilliant Friday

When coins jangle in trouser pockets,
And menfolk sit over jars of beer,
Staring into them long enough
To cause split sides of laughter.

Wednesday's a cosy sort of day,
Sitting squeezed in the middle,
Always enough and never too much,

A quiet sort of place, with just enough going off.

The Story of a Brick

The story starts with a brick
In a corner of this room.
I sit on it for a while.
It gets warm.

I paint it black.
I paint it white.
It's a big, square, rumbly cloud,
Then a station, waiting for people to come.
They all hurry on in.

One day it got added to a wall.
All the bricks were different.
All the bricks were the same.
I could have talked to any of them.
I just ran past when it rained.

Being Me Again

I'm only ever me, you know.
It's no good wanting to be you.
The hats won't change me nor daft clothes.
It's me inside still, through and through.

Sometimes I wave myself goodbye.
I walk away. I even run.
But something always drags me back
In the shape, sometimes, of mum,

Who makes me wash my face again
Or eat a sandwich before school.
I'm never hungry! I always say.
You will be soon, lad, I know your ways.

A King is a King

A king is a king
For a day or a moment
It depends on the horses
The hats and the coaches

A big one with rubies
A small one with jasper
Laugh as laugh can
They can only believe you

A king is a king
For a blink of a pleasure
It comes and it goes
Life never stops swinging

How big is the palace?
How small is the sadness?
A king is a king
For a puff of a moment

Balancing in the Air

There's nothing like
Balancing in the air
Long legs in the wind
Two arms spread like wings

There's nothing like being
As tall as the sky
With all to look down on
And people like flies

There's nothing like
Balancing in the air
With cloud puffs to rest on
When you feel tired

And rain clouds to sip from
When you are thirsty
And aeroplane people
To chat with when lonely

One Day

One day I was lost
In the middle of things
All tangled and messy
And tired and lonely

One day I was found
In a room with a view
With a friendly face talking
Of supper and you

One day I was lost
And no one could find me
And then I turned up
And you kissed me and hugged me

Never a never

Never a never
Always a something
A someone, a somewhere,
A place still to get to

How Many Miles

How many miles is far away?
Is it closer than nowhere?
Is it likely I'll get there
If I slip on my sandals
And hurry away
When it's still dark outside
And I don't know the way?

How many miles is quite near by?
Is it closer than Wendy?
Or softer than cushions?
Is it likely I'll get there
If I never stop looking
For daylight and sunshine
And favourite stories?

The Spell

You're not supposed to give out spells,
But *you* can have just one.
Now promise not to pass it on
To friend or foe or anyone.

This one's for turning ankles green
To make them glow at night
So that your feet can see to walk
When there isn't any light.

You mince up a toad in the Magimix,
And pickle a cat in wine,
Then you toss in a couple of dandelions
And a spoonful of turpentine...

What's wrong with you now?
Why're you looking like that?
You said that you wanted a spell.
I've given you one. It isn't a trick.

You look so peculiar. Oh please don't be sick.

My Sad Frend

I knew a witch who couldn't spell.
She lived at the bottom of a garden well.
I used to shout things down to her
(she was right miserable down there)

Like: why can't you magic yourself up?
It's warm where I live on the top...

Because I can't spel SPEL! she'd call.
Her voice was strange, so faint and small.
And if you can't spel SPEL, you're lost.
The magic just won't work at all!

Racing the Wind

I said to the wind — "I'll race you then
To that gate there And back again!"

But the wind said to me — "How will we tell
Which of us won? I'm invisible?"

So I thought and thought, And then I found
A crisp bag Crumpled on the ground.

I picked it up And said to the wind — "You blow this
And I'll just run..."

So off we went, Me and that bag
Dashing like mad, Not once looking back

But when we got there, The bag went on
Bouncing, flying

Right across The playing fields Till it got lost.

Well, I raced back To the starting line,
Shouting "I've won!

Your bag can't run In a straight line!"
The wind just didn't know

What to say. It huffed and puffed
And gruffed around,

Rattling the chimney pots all day, Blowing across and round and down,
Searching for that bag it lost...

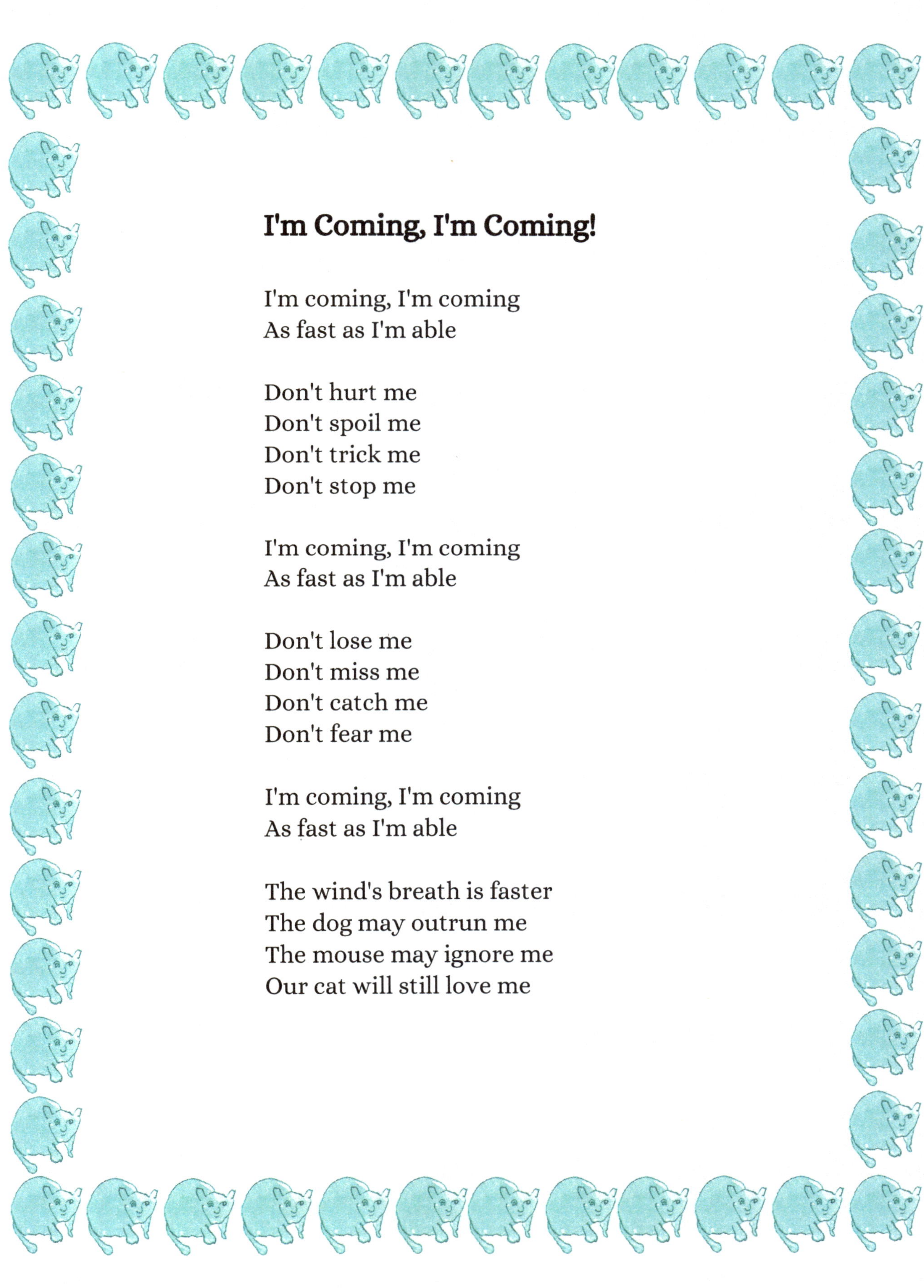

I'm Coming, I'm Coming!

I'm coming, I'm coming
As fast as I'm able

Don't hurt me
Don't spoil me
Don't trick me
Don't stop me

I'm coming, I'm coming
As fast as I'm able

Don't lose me
Don't miss me
Don't catch me
Don't fear me

I'm coming, I'm coming
As fast as I'm able

The wind's breath is faster
The dog may outrun me
The mouse may ignore me
Our cat will still love me

The Poetry
Room

The Room of You

Transform yourselves, dear children,
Into this Poetry Room that you are creating.

Let one of you be the planks of its floor,
Another the shining panes of its windows,
And a third the skimming height of its ceiling.

Now be careful what you do with yourselves.
Tiptoe quietly across the boards of your floor
So that you don't hurt yourselves.

Don't damage your delicate eyes by overlong looking
Into the distances that yawn from your window.

Most of all don't get dizzy by overlong lingering
At the height of your ceiling.

The Ceiling's Reply

And here is what the ceiling, a little crossly, is saying:

I, and not one of you (the poet is mistaken), am the ceiling.
I look down on you every minute of the day.
I hear every word that you whisper,
And I notice every time that you hesitate
And look here and there
because you have lost something.
I listen to all the songs that you sing
after supper in the evenings,
And I see when you have just combed your hair
before school in the mornings.

Frankly, I do not much care
if you are forever shouting and shouting
Because I will not be listening
to all the words that you will be using.
I am good at lying out flat all day and all night,
And this means that when the time comes to be asked —
And it will surely be coming —
I will be better than anyone at flying long distances
Without once stopping.

I suggest, dear children, that you learn from my example
By lying stretched out on the floor, arms spread,
And smiling up at me
Every night before you go up to bed
For about sixty-one seconds.

Travelling Across the Poetry Room

Today we travelled very far
Across the burning deserts of the floor
of this Poetry Room,
With our stores of water
and our seventeen tired, slow, dusty camels.

Now, at last, we have reached the window,
Where we are all allowed to rest and to sleep
In the cooling shade of the curtains.
I alone must stay awake —
the camels are already snortingly snoring through their thick lips —
In order to plan the long journey that is to take place

After breakfast in the kitchen with the children
When we will all, having washed, prayed
And given thanks for this night's safe haven,
Be required to proceed as far as the coast
In order to wait for the ancient boat
which will, in time, bear us all homeward
To our wives and seven hundred happy children.

Being the Window Pane

I sometimes wish I were not the glass panes of this window
Because someone — it was a brick, I believe — has just told me
That if they are not very careful,
These other children who are standing and staring through me,
I am liable to shatter.

And, frankly, what good will I be to myself and others in the future
If I am nothing more than one thousand tiny fragments?
For all that, let me try to stay cheerful.
Many people polish me until I shine proudly.
Others breathe on me with quick pantings of breaths,
Warming me on the coldest of winter mornings.
And someone kind and clever has even told me
That even if I do suffer the ultimate mishap of getting broken,
They can make me again,
And no one, not even I, will know any difference.

The Very Bigness of Our Poetry Room

I cannot enter this room because it is too big for me.
Don't be silly, you all tell me. It is not that big!
But it is.

Whenever I touch the walls, they step back from me and say:
This is only the beginning. You just wait!

When I climb the step ladder to the ceiling,
It rises and rises higher, then a little higher,
Just as I stretch up my arm to reach...

And then there is the awkward matter of the floor that starts
Just inside this door.
How low would you say that it was?
Is it as low as your feet?
No, you are wrong, it is not!
When I walk in the door, my feet fall away,
And then they keep on falling and falling
Until the end of this poem,

When everything stops,
And turns back to the room that it was
Before I entered it.
So who is to blame
That this room of yours is so strange?
Are you? Or is it me again?

Wake Me Up

Wake me up when I need to go.
I have decided to stay here all day
With my boxes of happy-go-lucky spoons, my several bananas,
And this cup of liquid gold in the shape and the taste
      of an ice cream.
You understand. You would not want to leave any of this too soon
For a slow day at school or a brisk day of walking,
      shivering, in the rain.

Naming The Walls of the Poetry Room

Each wall of this Poetry Room has a name of its own.
The left-hand wall is Oscar, the right-hand Richard,
And the other two, Fiona and Anne.
One day we will all do a dance, round and round,
Hand in hand, but not just yet.
We have not yet been introduced to each other.
We are so shy of each other's company just now
That we prefer to stay here in our places,
Never moving, never saying hello, not even to our neighbours.
Only you know our names, dear children.
Most people do not even know that every wall of this room is special,
And that each wall has its very particular name.
Do not forget us, but when you say our names out loud,
Please do so in a whisper.
The time has not yet come to tell all the others.

Stealing the Light from the Poetry Room

It is a dark day in the Poetry Room.
We are all crawling around on our hands and knees,
Looking for the word LIGHT.
During the night, someone came in here and stole it.
Who could have done such a thing?
When we open the books and look for it,
It is never in its proper place.
This book for example, begins 'switch on the... MISSING...'
Please help us to find it.
It is never too soon to find it.
Catch a train, take a bus,
Or fly here to help us
With your fires, your torches, your sunbeams and your candles.
All our books will remain invisible until we have found it.

It's Never Too Soon for the Poetry Room

It's never too soon
(No, it's never too soon)
For the walls and the ceiling and door
Of the Poetry Room!

It's never too soon
To stick poems and prose and much more
On the floor (and the ceiling and door)
Of the Poetry Room.

It's never too soon
In the morning, evening or at noon
To write poems to be hung —
or songs to be sung —
On the walls and the ceiling and door
Of the Poetry Room.

It's never too soon
To be Poetry Festival Time
When you scribble and rhyme
And speak out loud (at least three at a time)
In the ever expanding-with-fun-
At-least-just-as-far-as-the-sun
Space of the Poetry Room

The Silence of the Poetry Room

No one is in here now apart from myself.
I am the silence of the Poetry Room,
The ever thickening, ever deepening silence
Of the Poetry Room.
No one feels the gentleness of my footfalls.
No one hears the quality of my speechlessness,
So smooth to the touch and so soothing.
No one sees the breadth of my smile
    when it opens to the sunlight on a Saturday morning.
No one hears the song that I sing, so lullingly,
      to no one but myself.
No one knows what my silence means
    nor how much it weighs on this shelf.
So let me tell you — if you will agree to tell no one else.
My silence is the gap between one burst of laughter and another.
My silence is the sea's roar when you are deep underwater.
My silence is the sound of my tears when I am not yet crying.
My silence is the world's silence too
When all the voices of all the people,
All those singers and shouters and balloon-faced ranters,
Have finally vanished.

The Cupboard with Special Needs

I am unlucky to be this cupboard.
No one ever says to me: do you mind very much
If I put all this stuff in here?
Usually I say, yes I do. I mind quite a lot.
I am already full of last winter's shoes,
All so messily strewn about my floor.
I am already too hot with all the coats that hang here,
Jostling and jangling together on their hangers,
Always waiting, with very little patience,
For their turn to be used.

I am so full to the brim and beyond
That I cannot even make myself hear
When you stand in front of me with your boxes of toys
And your sacks of unfinished knitting.
I do not want to be pricked accidentally by your needles.

I am a proud cupboard, with very special needs.
Open me respectfully. Bow to me.
And if you really must fill me to bursting,
Please thank me for graciously allowing you
To do just as you please.

The Small Yellow Pencil

I am a small yellow pencil for building worlds out of words.
I sit upright in a jar with others of my kind, on this table,
Next to the rubber and the very useful empty labels.
Press very lightly when you use me.
You do not need finger pressure.
Instead, the door to be opened, you will quickly find,
Is just behind your eyes.
Open it gently. You will be in for a surprise.

There you will see them,
Mistily forming from your looking and looking
As you begin now to draw them,
All the worlds you will want to describe.
You will watch them, with much excitement, coming into being
On the paper you will be using
That someone gave you as a present, quite casually.
One world may be lonely, dark and as large as forever.
Another may be small, fussy and funny,
With several pelicans standing to attention
Near a cliff that could be frightening. Is it?
You will say to those pelicans:
Who brought you here? Will you live here forever?
They may laugh at you then. They may dance round you in a ring.
Your friend the cliff will now be echoing,
All day and all night, to your singing.

Closing the Door of the Poetry Room

Close the door of the Poetry Room.
It has been far too long open.
There has been too much noise and kerfuffle inside it,
Too many poems about jumping and laughter being written,
Too many poems being sung, acted and shouted.
Now it needs to rest just a little.
It needs to dream the dreams it will always be dreaming.
It needs to read for itself all the words you have used,
All the worlds you have conjured.
It laughs to itself when it reads them,
Oh how it laughs and it laughs
When you are so soundly sleeping.

Other publications by Michael Glover

Poetry:

Measured Lives (1994)
Impossible Horizons (1995)
A Small Modicum of Folly (1997)
The Bead-Eyed Man (1999)
Amidst All This Debris (2001)
For the Sheer Hell of Living (2008)
Only So Much (2011)
Hypothetical May Morning (2018)
Messages to Federico (2018)
What You Do With Days (2019)
One Season in Hell (2020)
The Timely Lift-Off of the Famous Harlequin-Fish (2022)
What Turns Up (2022)

Others:

Headlong into Pennilessness (2011)
Great Works: Encounters with Art (2016)
Playing Out in the Wireless Days (2017)
111 Places in Sheffield You Should Not Miss (2017)
Late Days (2018)
Neo Rauch (2019)
The Book of Extremities (2019)
Thrust (2019)
John Ruskin: an idiosyncratic dictionary (2019)
Rose Wylie (2020)
Whose? (2020)
Wingers and Leapers and Creepers (2021)
The Trapper (2021)
Nellie's Devils (2022)

As editor or contributor:

Memories of Duveen Brothers (1976)
Goin' down, down, down: Matthew Ronay (2006)
Between Eagles and Pioneers: Georg Baselitz (2011)
Robert Therrien (2016)
Monique Frydman (2017)
A Garland of Poems for Christmas (with Martyn Crucefix) (2022)